THE AMAZING ADVENTURES OF THE DC SUPER-PETS!

The Ice Cream Caper

by **Steve Korté**

illustrated by **Art Baltazar**

Batman created by Bob Kane
with Bill Finger

PICTURE WINDOW BOOKS
a capstone imprint

Published by Picture Window Books, an imprint of Capstone.
1710 Roe Crest Drive
North Mankato, Minnesota 56003
www.capstonepub.com

Cataloging-in-Publication Data is available at the Library of Congress website.
ISBN: 978-1-5158-7178-1 (library binding)
ISBN: 978-1-5158-7323-5 (paperback)
ISBN: 978-1-5158-7186-6 (ebook PDF)

Summary: Batman and his crime-fighting dog detective, Ace, investigate a robbery
at the Gotham City Zoo. Will the Caped Crusader and the Bat-Dog find out who is behind
the ice cream caper?

Designed by Ted Williams
Design Elements by Shutterstock/SilverCircle

Printed in the United States   4036

TABLE OF CONTENTS

He is Batman's
loyal friend.
He is a super-smart
crime-fighting canine.
He is known as the World's
Greatest Dog Detective.
These are . . .

THE AMAZING
ADVENTURES OF

Ace the
Bat-Hound!

CHAPTER 1

A Zoo Mystery

Batman zooms through the streets of

Gotham City in the Batmobile.

His loyal dog, Ace the Bat-Hound, sits beside him.

There was a robbery at the Gotham City Zoo. Batman and Ace are on their way to help.

"Someone stole all the penguins!" the zookeeper says.

"I wonder if the Penguin was here," says Batman. "Let's look for clues."

Ace sniffs a snowy area at the edge of the penguins' area.

He barks to get Batman's attention.

Batman joins Ace. Together, they study the wet ground. They see footprints from a man's shoe. There are pointy holes by some of the footprints.

"These holes look like they were made by the tip of an umbrella," says Batman. "The Penguin carries an umbrella. Excellent detective work, Ace!"

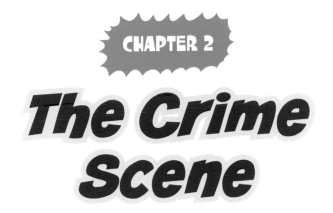

CHAPTER 2

The Crime Scene

Batman and Ace drive to a wide river.

A narrow bridge stretches across the

water. The Penguin's sinister hideout is

on the other side of the river. It looks

dark and scary.

"This bridge looks flimsy. It will never support the Batmobile," says Batman. "Ace, you stay here while I get out and look around."

Batman quietly enters the hideout.

Suddenly, he is ambushed! Two of the

Penguin's helpers tie up Batman.

Batman struggles to free himself.

The ropes are too tight.

The goons leave the hideout. They run across the bridge. They make it safely to the other side. Then they cut the ropes.

The bridge tumbles into the water. Laughing, the bad guys disappear into the woods.

Ace jumps out of the Batmobile. He runs to the edge of the river. The distance across is too far to jump.

The quick-thinking dog sees an old, tall tree nearby. The tree looks dry and dead.

Ace backs up and then takes a

running jump.

Ace's weight is enough to snap the

dead tree. It falls. Its trunk stretches

across the river.

Ace uses the tree like a bridge to cross the river. Then he crashes into the hideout.

Ace chews on the ropes around Batman. Soon the Caped Crusader is free!

CHAPTER 3

The Ice Cream Trail

The Bat-Hound sniffs the floor of the

hideout. He finds some spilled ice cream.

There are black feathers stuck in the

ice cream. Ace runs out of the building.

Batman follows him.

The trail leads to the Sweet Treats Ice Cream factory.

Inside the building, Ace and Batman find the Penguin. He has all the penguins from the zoo!

"The zoo exhibit was too warm," the villain explains. "I brought the penguins to a chilly place where they would be safe."

"You should not have stolen the penguins," says Batman. "But you did the right thing bringing them to a cold location."

The Caped Crusader thinks.

"Because you were looking out for the safety of the penguins, I'm going to ask the judge to give you a lighter punishment," Batman says.

In a courtroom two days later, the judge agrees with Batman. The Penguin is ordered to pay a large fine. The money will allow the zoo to build a better penguin enclosure. The Penguin must also spend time volunteering at the zoo.

JUDGE

25

Batman reaches down to pat his

loyal friend's head.

"Ace, it was your quick thinking that

solved this case!" says Batman.

"Woof!" says the World's Greatest

Dog Detective. He happily wags his tail.

AUTHOR!

Steve Korté is the author of many books for children and young adults. He worked at DC Comics for many years, editing more than 600 books about Superman, Batman, Wonder Woman, and the other heroes and villains in the DC Universe. He lives in New York City with his husband, Bill, and their super-cat, Duke.

ILLUSTRATOR!

Famous cartoonist Art Baltazar is the creative force behind *The New York Times* bestselling, Eisner Award-winning DC Comics' Tiny Titans; co-writer for Billy Batson and the Magic of Shazam, Young Justice, Green Lantern Animated (Comic); and artist/co-writer for the awesome Tiny Titans/Little Archie crossover, Superman Family Adventures, Super Powers, and Itty Bitty Hellboy! Art is one of the founders of Aw Yeah Comics comic shop and the ongoing comic series! Aw yeah, living the dream! He stays home and draws comics and never has to leave the house! He lives with his lovely wife, Rose, sons Sonny and Gordon, and daughter Audrey! AW YEAH MAN! Visit him at www.artbaltazar.com

"Word Power"

ambush (AM-bush)—a surprise attack

detective (di-TEK-tiv)—a person who investigates crimes or collects information for people

enclosure (en-KLOH-zhur)—an area closed in by a fence or wall

exhibit (ig-ZI-buht)—a display that usually includes objects and information to show and tell people about a certain subject

fine (FINE)—money a person must pay for breaking a law

flimsy (FLIM-zee)—weak or easily broken

hideout (HI-dowht)—a secret place for hiding

sinister (SIN-uh-stur)—looking evil or harmful

support (suh-PORT)—to help something

WRITING PROMPTS

1. Re-read the story. Make a list of all the clues Ace used to find the Penguin.

2. Draw a Wanted poster featuring the Penguin. What words would you use to describe him?

3. Make a timeline of the events in the story. Place events that happen in a shorter period of time close together. Leave more space between events that happen farther apart in time.

DISCUSSION QUESTIONS

1. The Penguin was trying to help the penguins stay cool by taking them to the ice cream factory. What other locations would have worked? Explain your reasoning.

2. What do you think would have happened to Batman if Ace hadn't been along?

3. Batman and Ace think the Penguin's hideout looks sinister. Do you think the Penguin would agree? Draw the hideout from the Penguin's point of view.